O CANADA
Our National Anthem

NORTH WINDS PRESS
A Division of Scholastic Canada Ltd.

O Canada!

Our home and native land!

True
patriot
love

in all thy sons
command.

With glowing hearts

we see
thee rise,

The True North strong and free!

From far and wide, O Canada,

We stand
on guard
for thee.

God keep
our land

glorious and free!

O Canada,
we stand on
guard
for thee.

O Canada,
we stand on guard
for thee.

O Canada

1880 — The tune that started it all...

The Music of Our National Anthem

It began with a melody.

Calixa Lavallée was born in 1842 in Verchères, Canada East (Quebec). Calixa's father was a blacksmith, but he also repaired instruments and led bands, so it is not surprising that his children were musical. At 13, Calixa travelled to Montreal to study piano, and when he was only 15, he left to play in the United States. During this time, his talents took him on a tour to South America, the Caribbean and Mexico. By the age of 30, he was back in Montreal. There he gave concerts as a pianist, violinist and cornettist, and was even given the opportunity to study in France for two years. When he returned, he opened a studio, gave concerts and travelled often to the United States.

It was at this point, in 1880, when Lavallée was 37 years old and a well-known musician, teacher and composer, that he was asked by the Lieutenant Governor of Quebec to compose a tune for an upcoming official banquet. He tried a number of drafts, until his musical friends greeted one moving melody with enthusiasm. It was the tune we know today. The story goes that in his excitement, he rushed off to show the sheet music to the Lieutenant Governor, and forgot to sign it.

1880 — Add the words, *en français*…
Our National Anthem in French

At the same time as Calixa Lavallée was working on his melody, the Lieutenant Governor made another request. He asked Adolphe Routhier to write a poem to go with the music Lavallée was creating.

Born in 1839 in Saint-Placide, Lower Canada (Quebec), Adolphe-Basile Routhier grew up to become a lawyer and a judge, as well as an accomplished and well-known poet. In 1880, when he accepted the invitation to write a poem for the banquet, he was the president of the *Congrès national des Canadiens-Français,* the very group that was holding the affair. The Lieutenant Governor's choice could not have been more perfect.

What Routhier created – *en français* – was "O Canada." The French lyrics of "O Canada" that we sing today are exactly those of the beautiful poem he wrote so many years ago. Not one word has ever been changed.

The song "O Canada," composed by Calixa Lavallée and with French lyrics by Adolphe-Basile Routhier, was first performed on June 24, 1880 before an audience of over 3000 people, at the banquet for the *Congrès national des Canadiens-Français* at the *Pavillon des Patineurs* (Skaters' Pavilion) in Quebec City.

1908 — At long last, the English version…
Our National Anthem in English

After that first performance in French, there is no record of any English version of "O Canada" for more than 25 years. Then, in 1906, a Toronto doctor translated the lyrics into English. In 1908, *Collier's Weekly* magazine held a competition to write an English text for the song. Several other English-language versions followed, including one written by the well-known poet Wilfred Campbell. But the simple words that really took hold were those written in 1908 by Robert Stanley Weir.

Weir was born in 1856 in Hamilton, Canada West (Ontario). He studied in Montreal and became a lawyer and a judge. As well as writing legal works, he wrote poetry. In 1908, when he was the Recorder of the City of Montreal, he wrote the English words to "O Canada," honouring the 300th anniversary of the founding of Quebec City.

These words were slightly modified and published in official form for the Diamond Jubilee of Confederation in 1927. Further changes to the first verse were recommended by a Special Joint Committee of the Senate and the House of Commons in 1968.

On July 1, 1980, one hundred years after it had first been performed in French, "O Canada" was proclaimed Canada's national anthem. And it was the first verse of Weir's poem that was declared the official English version. This is the song we sing today.

Scholastic Canada Ltd.
175 Hillmount Road, Markham, Ontario L6C 1Z7, Canada
Scholastic Inc.
555 Broadway, New York, NY 10012, USA
Scholastic Australia Pty Limited
PO Box 579, Gosford, NSW 2250, Australia
Scholastic New Zealand Limited
Private Bag 94407, Greenmount, Auckland, New Zealand
Scholastic Ltd.
Villiers House, Clarendon Avenue, Leamington Spa,
Warwickshire CV32 5PR, UK

National Library of Canada Cataloguing in Publication
O Canada : our national anthem.

English lyrics of the national anthem, accompanied by photographs of
Canada. Includes French lyrics and biographies of the composer, and
writers of both the English and French lyrics.
Issued also in French under same title.
ISBN 0-439-97457-7 (bound).--0-7791-1408-6 (pbk.)

1. Canada--Pictorial works. 2. Lavallée, Calixa, 1842-1891.
O Canada--
Juvenile literature. 3. National songs--Canada--Texts.

FC58.O2 2003   j917.1'0022'2
          C2002-905090-1
          F1008.2.O2 2003

Copyright © 2003 by Scholastic Canada Ltd.
All rights reserved.

6 5 4 3 2 1   Printed in Canada   03 04 05 06 07

Photography credits for O *Canada*

Cover: top left: Paul Isaac/Sunscape Design; top right: EyeWire Inc;
bottom right: PhotoDisc; bottom left: © Garry Black/Wonderfile.

Back Cover: Douglas E. Walker/Tourism Saskatchewan;
additional, paperback only, left: Image courtesy of Canadian Tourism
Commission; right: Stockbyte.

Page 2-3: Elizabeth Hak/Doodleshak Photography;
Page 4, left: Corbis; right: Comstock Images;
Page 5: ImageState;
Page 6: © Rommel/Masterfile;
Page 7, left/right: Images courtesy of Canadian Tourism Commission;
Page 8: Douglas E. Walker/Tourism Saskatchewan;
Page 9, left: Image courtesy of Canadian
Tourism Commission; right: Manon Pageau;
Page 10: © Bill Clarke;
Page 11: Corel
Page 12: © David Cattanach/Painet Inc;
Page 13: © Mirrorlock Photography;
Page 14: Image courtesy of Canadian Tourism Commission;
Page 15, left: Corel; right: EyeWire Inc;
Page 16, top: Comstock Images; bottom: © Mirrorlock Photography;
Page 17: Image courtesy of Canadian Tourism Commission;
Page 18: Image courtesy of Canadian Tourism Commission;
Page 19, top © John Sylvester Photography; bottom: © J.A.
Wilkinson/Valan Photos;
Page 20: © John Sylvester Photography;
Page 21, left: AbleStock; right: © 2002 Heiko Wittenborn;
Page 22: AbleStock;
Page 23: Stockbyte;
Page 24, left: © Niall Benvie/Nature Picture Library;
right top/bottom: Images courtesy of Canadian Tourism Commission;
Page 25, left: Pat Kramer;
centre: © www.PerfectPhoto.ca/Rob vanNostrand; right: Corel
Page 26-27: © Jean-Guy Lavoie/Tourisme Québec;
Page 29, left: National Archives of Canada;
right: From the collections of the Music Division of the
National Library of Canada;
Page 30: National Library of Canada;
Page 31: Matthew Farfan Collection.

Page 28: Music typeset by Trevor P. Wagler/Flamingo Soup Music
Publishing and Productions, Inc.